THE GLOBE OF UNCANNY

DECENT RELISH

SUMEET KUMAR

ISBN 979-888569693-7

Sumeet Kumar

Sumeet Kumar , A adult who experiences many phases of love in his life , get broked many times , stands up every time and keep moving to the next phases of the life.In reality he is a writter as well as singer (as a hobby). Very exciting and interesting fact about him is that he is aauthor of New era i.e. he starts his journey of writing at the age when he was going to schools to get the study . His some famous works i.e. Maturity Of Love (Genre - Love),Privacy For Dream (Genre - Middle Class), Army Squad ofLove (Genre- The Seperation of Army Love), 5 Days of Love(Genre- Temporarily Love), Th e Endearment Of Love(Genre - Historical Era Of Love), Social Destruction Indo-Pak (Genre - The Story of The Love At The Time Of Division Of India And Pakistan), Middle Class Soul (Genre - The Dreams of Middle Class), The Accursed Kanatpur (Genre -The Horrific Story Of A Village), Wrong Number (Genre -The Suspenseful Physco Killer Story), The Secrecy OfDeadly Midnight (Genre - The Suspense About a Crime),Fragile Religious Of Death (Genre- The Death Of A TrustfulPerson), Nature Vs Science (Genre - The Future Battle Between Nature And Science In A Horrific Way), Generic Man (Genre - The Dream of I.I.T), The Unconsious 12 Hours(Genre - The Illusion At Stage Of Comma), The StrangeBurden (Genre - The Burden Of Love) , Her Existence (Genre- The Female Pain In The Society) , Jockstrap Prize (Genre -The True Story Of A National Athlete) , H Man [Hindi] (Genre - Superhero Tragic Story), H Man [English] (Genre - Superhero Tragic Story) , Maturity Of Love [Englsih] (Genre - Love) and many more are available on various geners on the offcial platform of **Amazon, Flipkart and Notionpress.** You can buy them from there.

Contents

ACKNOWLEDGEMENTS

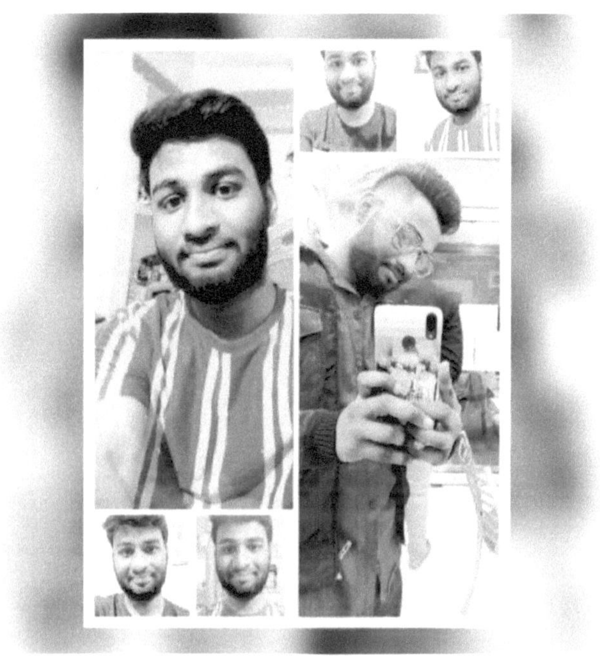

Aman Kumar

Special Thanks to **Aman Kumar** who worked so hard in the preparation of this book. He has continually put with my passive voice, omission of words, and late night calls. You have be en wonderful. Thanks to him for his precious time in reviewing proposals , individual chapters and early drafts, along with his suggestions on the applicability of the material to the world.

I
Evidence Of Time

When the relationship becomes an accident, then they start giving trouble because in reality, every one-sided conversation that we do for each other is only a show-off. Only the walls are made, if someone has seen the reason for pain in the gathering, then he must have seen the moments of peace. If he is not in a relationship then he seems to be deserted, among them whom we never even say to see, if a witness is in love with another person, then why should he need a third person to tell his heart? Not that he cannot express the image of his alpha in front of his love I am not able to rock my feet in the gathering, because of which I can rock it, the candles of love It is in some way that we must say vows to be together for a few moments. To play the feet, the old age is also a work party, which is also afraid of losing the witness, if he falls in love with someone, then it is also the beginning of his love. Right now the politics of the path is good, well, there is no request to do the slave of the daughters before the time, There is a lack of experience in life, I know that I have played true love with everyone. I have gone ahead, why am I saying these things, I do not know myself because I have never accomplished anything in my life, like this, even though I have some kind of happiness, I am very difficult, society says time With the help of my feet, I am suffering from the pain of training and the pain, which is the reason for the work and there is a new in me. Is making space to keep myself safe. Why do I keep silent all the time to fall in love with the abuses I hate so much.

> *"Before Ending of this journey*
> *I want to request*
> *Don't make me a part of someone*
> *because i am very weak in maintaining the*
> *relationships."*

Age has no life, feet is a bailout is necessary, if any evidence makes you love yourself too much I have seen myself becoming famous with my eyes. You are wrong then why do I feel like this because I keep myself away from his eyes, why I needlessly ask to run away from his friends everywhere and keep myself safe because I don't even want to live again. Why do I keep the charity alive all the time? I ask her only one question every time was she right what was wrong with her

People say that if you are in love with one age, it is okay if you become a lover with one age, then that is also fine. love then is kind of thingh which repel the haters of the world and nor male people then it will be or nor male thats kind of generation then it will be due to which we make our sleep the whole night the reason for our ruin for a meeting. It is said that when a witness starts getting suffocated from a gathering, then he At the same time, I should say goodbye to the male gathering, my life had become a suffocation in my part. That every lamp is silence and exhaust , which weakens me all the time, makes me feel that I am wrong even though I am right? Then they live together for a few moments and after that they take away from each other, do they give the name of love

"Because I know no emotion, no society,
he said about me with great ease.
Said that we are both exactly the same."

What is the fault of those relationships, who do not even know why they associate one witness with another witness, there are many such people in the world who are said to be aware of the love of anger, because the love of others who has Love begins and the body ends even if everything is necessary in the world, then love is also necessary because if the witness is incomplete, then only his love can fulfill it. Yes, because self-love is also very wonderful. There are some people who forget their own love in the same abuses, where even their death has no value, I am going to tell some such things about myself. Whom all of you know, may have started feeding hatred towards me. It does not happen when people meet each other, they have conversation between them then they get to know each other very well. I am saying this because it is a twilight , it is a fantasy, people think about each other, expect each other's feet, Until then, they are not complete, in reality, there is no bigger and incomplete thing than love in the world, how are relationships formed, This question is, I must be making some different kind of pickles in all of you? Relationships are those people who don't talk about their locality, everyone says to stay on their feet, I know that no one among you will be coming to the society, that's why I am comparing relationships with Sehar Sehar. The feet are right, so I said about the relationship, these people live like a stranger, the feet would be like ignorant, so the feet where the gathering is deserted, happiness will surely be found in the part of the sorrow, in reality, the truth of the relationship would have been a hope.

Hope, which we call to see when we find a reason to make ourselves happy, unnecessarily people take each other's feet. It seems that I can even become a grave for your love pan, why people say to each other that I have done a lot to save our relationship, I have given you every time that I can keep for myself. This is a question that I asked all those who do not have that relationship in reality It is my mother-in-law that I have done this for you, I am doing that for you. I have given up everything for you. It is never true to the relationship, not the moments that you have spent together, the memories that come together You take care of each other by giving it the name of an accident, if those relationships cannot be seen, then why do they do false promises and promises to fulfill in front of each other, why I love the world of a farce You take it and go ahead and give it the name of a relationship that you can never handle People are in love to fill a lie Why do we take the help of only those who live with great pride in their gathering even after giving thousands of sorrows, they do not suffer, people move ahead in their lives, it all says that the feet are truthful, even today it is important that no one moves forward. Bash time's relationships change, that too in exchange for happiness and sorrow, relationships are never played one sided, just like true love of someone, if one pain is health, then the other also gives pain to himself after seeing his pain. Requests that if one is happy for some reason, then he was looking for many reasons to include the other in his happiness, but love is not the only party to bear many squabbles, to get it, then he went somewhere in a relationship. is formed.

> *"I don't want to go into those abuses and repeat*
> *the mistakes again*
> *She is so happy with his friends*
> *so I don't want to show my face again."*

Well, the education of talk is enough for this chapter, if I express my words more than this, then those who are going to listen to my story should be troubled, so the talk has been ended here. It started and maybe you can even name it as love, I think it can't be love and why can't it be, you can see for yourself.

II
Damages Everything and Everywhere

If life is bright, then the hope of living increases a bit, the reality is that at the time of their dreams, they start getting worse, life has become a habit for everyone. Why did I become like this and who made me like this, to run after a person's reason? It is said that a family keeps something together, never tries to break it, if someone is very weak in some family, then it does not mean that it is not a gift. To you card him separately, it doesn't even mean that if he is wrong, then forgive him at any time. My life was probably not just the writing of things, that's why they didn't even give me a chance It is not with me because maybe I have left my own journey and have separated myself from all the means of living, now there are also things to say Reminds me of the silence which I do not ask to see, nor do I ever say to share about it, I was wrong, these people understand that even those who gave birth to me feel good about me How right and how wrong these batis are, it will be known only after knowing the whole story, so let's hear that unheard story in which every wall of pain was broken, which I used to think for myself. So this story is a good place from which I Was quite ignorant, maybe that city on that time for me was quite well-versed, that means this story is from KANPUR , the one in whose name is hidden his passion, I do not mean to say that people like to listen too much, I mean to say this That it's good enough, maybe it's love is nothing special in ARUN PATHAK , a boy from such a house where his principles were everything for him, in a way, he was his life Can't win nor can you get any kind of respect Feet is one thing that you can achieve and it will never go away from you. Honesty is my own happiness, this is my wish Even for the time being, they say that even if wealth and children come in front of the principle, then without thinking anything, we should keep our principles in front and keep everyone behind. This was our father's manna, I had also learned from childhood, how right and wrong these conversation were, my brother was never aware of it Neither it had gone against my family nor did I have any hope of knowing what to do I am young, I am neither a habit nor a habit, sometimes it gets smaller, which kind of conversation father used to say, from time to time till today. Now the heart doesn't even ask why it can't be that she is also wrong and I am right, I am wrong in the eyes of the world and why is she right? such things always used to speak to his mother. Not only that, every thing which related to achievements of father was true, he had made me feel by choosing his principles, he could not separate himself from himself even after choosing his love in front of him. The whole story will also be left incomplete like my relationship, when the story started, this incomplete story started when I met KANAK on that way as a imaginary angle for the first time, she was very different from the rest of the girls, her beauty, her love, her thinking and everything The rest of the girls were very different, I had seen only one glimpse of her at the time and I was completely mad after her in the happy glimpse Then, by the way, let me tell you that she was the daughter of my father's friend VIKRANT UNCLE . In reality, he was very strict and why not even live, after all, who was a COLONEL , let me tell one more thing that my dad and Vikrant uncle were They were very good friends because both were classmates of childhood and they grew up together, feet might not have written the same thing in their fate, so both were Indians, so how could there be any other thing in their mind other than justice in their blood? Maybe. I don't have the same strength to keep my country safe as much as the limit is inside our military brothers. Doesn't say or was ready for them to talk about living in front of them neither when I knew what a relationship is like?

*"Some were now near death in my most beautiful parts of life
who is in the grave the life
asking these was her grace in my dreams were undefined"*

III

Smile Disappears

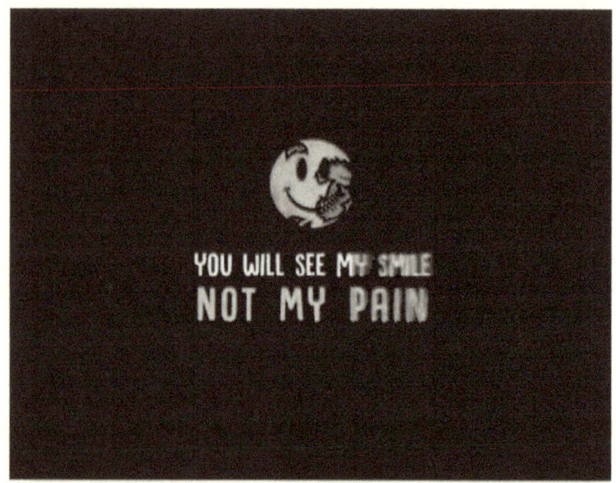

There are some such relationships in the world, which even without saying anything, we get attached to us, from which we can never be separated and even if we try to separate, then we ourselves become silent in their office that At the time, we forget our own existence, perhaps some similar relationship was going to be formed between me and Kanak, which was neither at the time nor I did not tell me that I should be tied in such a ritual which I I never tried my feet, everyone tried a lot and they would have been successful at some point. My love was never to join those relationships, so I did what I didn't want to do. Dad and Vikrant uncle did both of us. Without asking, the marriage of both of us had been fixed. I can't understand it, I had already said that this story has never been completed, it is such an incomplete story that I did not tell to complete it at the right time and probably still not. I say to do because after all whatever we both felt, maybe something was not right for both of us. The bride was ready because both of us had fallen in love and with whom we may have never met her. Loved himself more, nor did Kanak ever meet a male boy whom he himself loved more Never said anything about each other's love because we ourselves did not even know at that time that the one we love is the one who is finally It is time for Muhurat to call Kanak and Arun, and when Pandit ji is also speaking about the pending marriage culture , they have said that both of them are calling soon. Oh they are fine, you worry, I see in Anirudh how, Tells them that the bridegroom has missed the part of Then ,when ? leaving his bride behind his love affair, whom he has never met till date, only met him in dreams, in reality in life So her wicks had become the support of my life and it was my story like a bride, the same story, just like the handwriting of each one, like this, our handwriting was also exactly the same, we both came out together I had feet without telling each other that too in the name of my future husband, leaving a character in the name of his future wife. There must have been some kind of accident of fate, the love of both of us was also the same and the love was also the same, the only difference was that both of us were not the same, the letters we had written to each other's names, When letter now He was a reader, who probably did not even know about the thing, I had already said that father was very sure of his principles for him. Family came later and their emotions came later, before that their principles used to come first, that day something similar happened as soon as dad read that letter, he didn't let anyone say anything at the time, enough picked up my photo and Yes ! where we were going to giggle together, that too life happy and dad gave me pulses in pieces with my picture and Vikrant uncle also said that he was going to sit quietly, after all those friends who were they also did what their friend told me Did together means took Kanak's photo and cut it into pieces with him and gave lentils in fire , well, we are not married, if we see one way, then it would have happened that the feet were not ours, that too our pictures. One more thing in each other's day was that marriage is not only a match of two souls, but also matching of two pictures can lead to marriages. After each day neither my father searched for me nor Never tried to find out the reason, nor did he narrate to adopt the son back, he had said on the same day that now we have only one beta who was my brother. that day was neither special for anyone , it jus a bad deprived day ,mother nor anything said to dad then nor to anyone else because he knew who was important to him if he had supported me, he might have been in my place too, feet Vikrant uncle didn't do anything like that Am he had given pictures of Kanak in my life, he was not my dad's eighteen at all. Never told because he thought that he would refuse, every soldier has a heart inside him, he also has those feelings, he says not to express it in front of anyone because he cares about his country nothing like this happened. Kanak's dad means Vikrant uncle tried to find him a lot Didn't even know that the feet say that if someone wants to meet in luck, then they meet many times in the same birth, now in our story they come and go.You will not only be surprised by numbing it, instead you will all become a fan of such a fantasy which is called confusion in common language.

""For which fly i have been trapped in royality ,
Neither a traveller is seen
Nor any hope of getting success is seen""

IV
Unusual State Of Mind

Many accidents in a day in the world, some accidents are right, some accidents are wrong and some accidents are such that they do not take the name of losing our hearts and minds and say this with me at the same time. There were some accidents of heart and mind with both of them, meaning we were running away from some thing, after all the same thing had come in front of us and how did it come? And when it came, all of you yourself can see it with your lovely eyes. Something like this happened in a young day and Kanak that had parted the ways for each other's love ,and for each other's love, luck might not have accepted this thing even at this time that we should never fall in love with each other, all of you It is requested that please do not misunderstand the opposite thing, I mean I used to love that girl, from whom I first got my foot on social networking site I forgot one thing to tell you all What was the name of the social networking app which made the relationship between both of us so sure that we were left on the same foot with each other, that too for the whole life, this incomplete life was also the name of the thing. You will know only after seeing the accidents ahead, I forgot my name again, I didn't even tell you the name of the social networking app, like it, "add the relationship and break the sourness" I know that you all feel the same after listening to the name of the app." It must be surprising that as long as I was hot, it means that it is not a name but the latch of the family, when I first heard the name of the app, that too from a male witness who has not married till today. I cannot request it now or else the mention of those accidents may be left incomplete in my words, which was neither acceptable to me to a large extent nor Kanak's day when we both left our own marriage for someone and for the sake of our home and family. After sacrificing our respect, when we came out to him, he had come to Goa directly, that too looking for her because when we last talked between ,means realated to our last on conversation , then I asked her if we can meet because if I want to meet you Couldn't find it now, I'll probably never be able to find it, that's why she told me to come to Goa, he also gave an address which I can remember It's not even my foot I wrote it was wrong, Golden Tulipgo Candolim, enough I only know that she called me here I have never met her, I have never seen her before, nor have she ever seen me, how can there be love with only alphabets and words? Honestly, people do love in the world only through words, I mean to say It is that body is only a means of reuniting any two lovers and my love lights were also something like this, it is said that in life you ask for one thing, you ask for your share every day and that if you If she doesn't get it, his request also ends with time and he didn't even say that I didn't try to see her, she used to tell her not to look at her, she used to tell her not to see the unknown right beautiful eyes, his happiness and his that. smile used to say to see everything with his own eyes, when he gave up his mind, I had also thought that now whenever I meet her . If I will, I will say to get it for my whole life, this long relationship is also amazing, there is no idea when the love becomes deeper It is different, I know that I did not say at all that I should meet such a witness whom I have never seen nor felt the existence of both of us and suddenly when I fall in love with the witness, then in my dreams Even the visible dreams seem to be real, the meeting of both of us was not a dream, it was a fate in which both of us had tied so much that I was ready to do anything for him. I love her, will she also be in love with him the same way? If you do, it is not necessary that you should also request happy things from a witness if you are from any witness. If you are very much in love, then in return, he also loved you as much, it was not necessary that I knew that our conversation are not a show, our emotions are not a joke about each other, yet somewhere inside the heart these lamps are not It was also that it was just a fantasy, I did not say that the person who had missed my whole world for a few moments, without even seeing it, he started looking like the moon of the day, because only the rays of the sun are there in the day. not like the moon, the man who is already a slave to the darkness.

"The God has lost some part of the my pain
but you are still a wish for me to live
If you're not able to fill my wish , then give the
death sentence to my life."

After all I had paid the pouch where she called, I don't remember anything about the day's bailout because the way I ran in front of my family's eyes, at the time I had only two clothes and a ticket and some money. Anyhow, he asked, he went, Vikrant uncle was not only misting his daughter Kanak, he was also looking for me somewhere because I had seen his men at the railway station feet, who were asking every time they came. You have seen the deck of the groom, meaning you have seen the boy, Who asks such a picture of me from work to work I forgot that my father burnt my all pictures while sleeping Had given that too in a happy event where I was going to take a walk, that too with my dear friend. taht conversation was missing and his smile every time times! Only Sam was looking at me, the man had lost his time in his own eyes and regrettably, the heart had crossed the limit to some extent. So the phone itself was being switched off I thought he would be very angry with me that's why she had switched off his phone and even if she had to tell the truth then why would she be deceiving even in front of her? I could say no feet, no such things never come to my mind, I am a donkey, she says absolutely right about me that I can never take any right decision. Even in half the journey of meeting my love, the time was not special for me, I felt that Kanak is angry right now, so what happened I will consider her as soon as I meet her, then what was my love train had left That too on his way to his feet, where there was no such turn at the time, in the enough and his friends were with me. Time was traveling with me. Well, it is said that there are some accidents in life, about which we do not realize the time, nor have any experience, how can we handle it ,Now some similar accidents in my life too I was about to come, who was unaware of the happy times, had no idea that all this was going to happen to me that the thing that I was running in the eyes of the witness, finally my meeting will be happy.

> *""Missing her everytime , Remembered only her*
> *words but can't even say how i became well*
> *I didn't know how my eyes and ears will see*
> *and hear his glimpse and voice again.*
> *Everytime her voice is heard in my dreams*
> *again and again.""*

Means why do these accidents happen with me, why do I share them with me, why do not I get a ladder in my life even without saying why I am facing my father's words after that, then the teacher's words and now why am I facing her Why can't I all live a simple right life in such a confusing life if it was only then why the above person choose me, why couldn't anyone else choose someone else for this if they had to mix then at any time And why didn't he get the meeting, why he was the only witness in front of whom I would neither be able to express anything nor speak anything, well, whatever is going to happen in front of me, I am not only responsible for it, but there is someone else in its place. One who is a part of the equality, then goes ahead and sees some news about the guilty and what crime did he commit, but he also turns his eyes a bit .

V
The Fight Of Possession

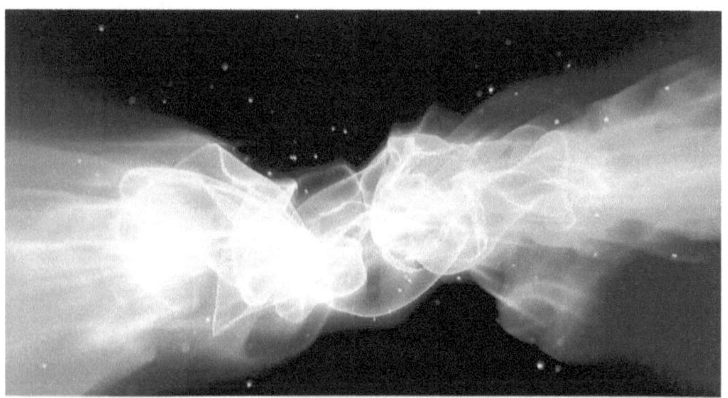

There are some moments in our life, which we never
say never to hurt our friends, we used to say to do in the
feet because now I was about to make a new beginning,
that too with the witness with whom I used to fall in love
without knowing that Because of my education decision,

many people's hearts would be broken, what should I do when someone is truly in love, then neither the family is visible nor the family lights. Jishne saw many such moments in front of my eyes, where only happiness's family has given happiness, it was not at all such a thing that I did not remember that face of my father, I did not remember his bati, all the yards were in my dreams at the time. Men didn't say to bring time, in the world, if we have true love for someone, then they only love themselves and I started feeling it when I left my family's clothes in the same abuses of Kanpur where I had come. Every single childhood memory is visible to every love of my family, because of which I have never lost my life. There is no pain in life, the feet are in love, there is something like this, neither love nor any friendship is seen in it, nor does society come in the society at the time. Before this I had already expressed this that I was about to get a man's love, which he neither asked to see nor had any request to meet me, it was not a matter of meeting me, I hated male witness, the thing was that I do not say to face my past, that too my future In front of me, something happened that as soon as I asked Goa to meet a male witness whom I had never met, it meant that we both fell in love with each other only in alpha. Those childhood memories of my family, Kanpur, my home and my dearest friend's heart had already been broken long ago, that too for just a glimpse of her, it was not that I was in love with her face because till today I have never seen her. Didn't get it, so how can I be in love with my face, not myself, why did I come to Goa? For me, I had toaded the walls of love, which I never told to break, I don't know how my feet were not feeling for sometime Those baatis, their yaadis, every single moment in my mind I was asking this question all the time why did you do this , what was the need, everything was going well, I didn't even know myself why I did this I was so happy that it would be better if we didn't meet the axis today, because neither will I be able to give him the happiness that he knew before with the help of two-sided bats, in the bash he could somehow return to the sixth leg. It was not even the approval of my heart at the time that I should go away from her. If it is done then we should look for a new way and I had only my clue when, after waiting for a long time, when he If she didn't come, I had taken it that like her lamps, her every existence is a sham and nothing else because even the house of time had changed right from time to time, it was going to be morning to evening. Didn't message nor call, I went to the society to say that I was explaining to myself that I am wrong, my love is wrong, every person is wrong, feet say that when you are very close to your destination in life, so many Accidents try to break you and in my life another accident was going to happen in my life. She was someone else only Kanak. I am not able to understand anything. By giving a new picture of an unfaithful to her lover after defeating her, then only then she massages me that where have you come I can't see my broken feet Ho I would have asked him many questions at the time that he was so late, you said I was different, you were not only because I was going to break , I do not say that at all, I was very happy because The paths that I had chosen were probably right for some time and those paths were also of some importance so that neither our relationship was ever going to break nor would I ever fall again in the eyes of my family because? There was no one else but Kanak was there, I know all of you were very surprised at the time, she was not good enough, there was someone else with her whom I used to do, due to which I had fallen in love in two moments, for which I got home and family. And he was ready to leave the abuses of Kanpur, right now my whole life is very complicated. After all, what is going to happen next in my life? Will that girl of Kanak whom I used to share, if she is, then he will be with her. Who is the other girl and why are they both asking about Abhiraj and who is this Raj right now? Whatever things you all will soon know, till then you should also try to understand the gift of some unfinished moments in my life and give me some time to understand too

""I have heared from her Beautiful Silence , Feet of her heart, Don't Break me
She always has a question even today why did you hold me
But the feeling of today questions from me
Why she had promises the lie everytime to me.
""